Gag

Based on Actual and Imaginary Events

by Stephen Schwegler

GAG

© 2014 Stephen Schwegler
ISBN: 978-0692308684

Published by Trees and Squids

TREES AND SQUIDS PUBLISHING
Albuquerque, New Mexico
www.treesandsquids.com

<u>Praise</u>

"Amazing, stupendous, and a whole host of other positive adjectives. *Gag* is an engrossing and cathartic ride, all too familiar to anyone who's been too close to the edge."

- Eirik Gumeny (Exponential Apocalypse series)

"Raw, funny, and just plain weird, *Gag* is a fictional memoir from a unique thinker and immensely talented writer. Schwegler's doing honest work, showing readers what it's really like to live with mental illness."

- Chris Rhatigan (The Kind of Friends Who Murder Each Other)

"This man put together a bunch of words. Those words made sentences. Those sentences formed chapters and those chapters told a story. And then those chapters got drunk and told the story again. And then those chapters got sober and told the story about how they accidently told that first story twice. There are moments of real emotional rawness in here, though they are stitched together by scenes painted in absurd colors. The repetition of the story is actually rather effective, showing how the same scenes, presented in various orders, can strike an unexpected chord of sincerity. Or levity. Or insanity. Perhaps that's the real take-away here. Anxiety makes life unpredictable, even when you're treading somewhere as familiar as your own house. As you're walking through the living room of this book for the third time, you suddenly realize you're still unsure of how it will all unfold. The furniture keeps getting rearranged. You keep tripping over ottomans like the opening credits to the **Dick Van Dyke Show**."

- Danger Slater (DangerRAMA)

Also by Stephen Schwegler

Perhaps.

Scattered Together

Screw the Universe (with Eirik Gumeny)

For the panicked masses

From the Desk Inside the Mind of the Author

So, here's the thing. This book is actually set up as three smaller stories. Hold on, don't go anywhere. I'm not done yet. Each one tells the same general story, but with different chapter sequencing and mood. This is why there are no chapter numbers, only titles. So yes, you will be reading the same text three times.

The reasoning behind naming this book *Gag* was due to "gag" being a palindrome and homonym. "What does that have to do with anything?" you might be saying. Let me explain.

You can think of the first version out of the three as being a palindrome. I've titled this one "Despair."

The next is "Dependence," which is actually the previous version in reverse chapter order.

The last one, "Desire," is a jumbled up one. If you refer to "Despair" you will see that this third version essentially reads as chapter 1, 9, 2, 8, 3, 7, 4, 6, 5.

The homonym connection comes from each chapter title also being one.

Gag is an extremely personal tale of my own panic attacks and anxiety. A lot of it is based on real events. And a lot of it is completely made up.

Gag:

Verb:

: to put something (such as a piece of cloth) into or over a person's mouth in order to prevent that person from speaking, calling for help, etc.

: to prevent (someone) from speaking freely or expressing opinions

: to vomit or feel as if you are about to vomit : to feel as if what is in your stomach is going to come up into your mouth

Noun:

: something said or done to make people laugh

: something done as a playful trick

: something (such as a piece of cloth) that is put into or over someone's mouth in order to prevent speech

-"Gag." *Merriam-Webster.com*. Merriam-Webster, n.d. Web. 27 Oct. 2013.

ACCOUNTS

Despair	Dependence	Desire
Recess	Rash	Recess
Reel	Faint	Rash
Whip	Whip	Reel
Zest	Fray	Faint
Balance	Balance	Whip
Fray	Zest	Whip
Whip	Whip	Zest
Faint	Reel	Fray
Rash	Recess	Balance

Despair

RECESS

Complete darkness. Ah, just me and my thoughts. That is until that blasted sun shows up and takes a bright luminescent shit on everything. And here he comes now.

I'm standing on some sort of mountain watching some kind of creature flying around some point in the distance. I patiently wait for my chance to strike because that's what you do in these situations. Right? I hear its shrill screech as it starts to become clearer. I leap into action.

I misjudge the jump and miss the creature completely. During the fall I manage to turn myself around and finally get a decent look at the flying abomination I've been tussling with up here on the cloud-engulfed rock.

"A fucking dragon?" I say, still falling to my imminent death. "Nope! I'm out."

"Grrrowl?" asks the dragon as it dives after me.

"Back, you flying lizard!"

"Hey there, hold on a second" it says. "You can't use the L word! That's our word."

"Shit, sorry," I say, "I had no idea. I meant no disrespect by it."

It replies, "While I believe that you were not aware of its derogatory nature making this all a silly little coincident, but I will have to beg to differ with you, my good man."

"Huh?"

"You see," the dragon continues, "while you didn't know you weren't a'supposed to say that word, ya did mean some disrespect."

One doesn't normally see a dragon turn into a little gumdrop pony, but there it is. Right in front of me. At this very minute. Man, I wish I had a camera.

"Hey!" squeaks the adorable, yet edible, gummy pony prancing about my feet. "We were having a conversation, Mister-I-don't-give-two-shits-about-what-you're-saying-so-I'm-going-to-look-off-in-the-distance-with-the-dumbest-look-on-my-face—"

"I guess I did kind of space out there for a mini—"

"And now you're interrupting me too! I should smite you down to the depths of Hell to pathetic little imp. I'll grind your bones to dust and sprinkle them on top of just some of the most diabetes-inducing cupcakes your twinkling peepers ever did see, Fuckface."

Okay. I'm frozen in terror and pee. Mostly pee.

"What just happened there?" I ask.

"Oh, that," says the I-don't-know-what. "I change shape randomly. Major fuckin' ball ache, let me tell you!"

"So what are you supposed to be now?"

"Fuck if I know. This is your brain after all. As far as I can tell you either took a LOT of hallucinogens or..."

"Or what?"

"Or you're really fucked up in the head."

"Oh, it's the latter."

"Ya think?"

"Oh totally. I stopped taking acid like weeks ago."

"Fantastic!" said the anthropomorphized bicycle hovering in front of me. "Also, why do I have the urge to ask you to hop on me and move your feet around?"

"You're a bike."

"I see."

"You're hovering though, that's cool.

The bike released some tire pressure.

"Did you just fart?"

"I think I did."

Now it's a flying bookcase with every Science Fiction book ever written on it.

"So... Now you're a bookcase," I pronounce astutely.

"Not just any bookcase," says the furniture using a voice that brings to mind images of ghosts and goblins, "but a magic Sci-Fi one! I'm going to go off and read a few of these before I turn into the Queen of England's vibrator. Oh, how terrifying."

It's flying away now. Come to think of it, I'm flying as well. Wasn't I falling a little while ago? Where the fuck am I?

I land safely on the floor that just happen to appear from out of thin air and can't seem to find anyone who might know what's happening.

I hear a voice slither into my ear and say, "What about that bookcase dude? He was pretty cool."

"I looked, but I can't even find him now."

A slight buzzing rolls in from off in the distance. A couch appears. A woman of considerable age is facing the opposite direction. The buzzing suddenly stops. She rests her head back.

As I, quite rapidly, adjust my position from vertical to something more horizontal, a flick of what must be a lighter shatters the silence. As the darkness slowly creeps in, the faintest trail of smoke rises above her crown.

REEL

Morning again! Awesome! Another day where I don't get to go anywhere because they're out there. With their prying eyes and judgmental... brains! For the love of... What the Hell is wrong with me?

"I can help you with that question," says a voice that I'm not one hundred percent sure is actually real.

"And who might you be?" I ask, actually expecting a response.

"I am you..."

Great.

"From a different dimension," the voice continues.

"I see. You wouldn't have anything to do with the insanely large vat of anxiety pills I took before, would you?"

"Perhaps."

"Right. So, if you don't mind. I'd like to go about my day. I have a busy schedule of watching cartoons and glaring out the window at all of the well-adjusted people going about their normal lives and so forth. You know. Work and shit."

"I'm sorry, sir. I didn't know you had so much on your plate," says the voice while finally taking the physical form of me, but dressed in a top hat and tails.

"Holy fuck," I literally say to myself. "Even I want to whack myself in the nuts. Why the hell am I dressed like that?"

"Just thought it was the thing to do," said my other-worldly self, almost imitating Jacob Marley's inflection from one of the televised Dickens productions.

"Uh huh."

"Care to dance, sir?"

"Why are you calling me 'sir?' We're the same person. I shouldn't be a higher class than you. For fuck's sake man, I'm stoned out of my gourd. Wait. Did you just ask me to dance?"

"Indeed I did, sir. Around the fountain, perchance?"

Well I'll be a... robot's antenna, I don't know. My bedroom now has a fountain in the middle of it. Not to mention the four-piece string section that magically appeared out of nowhere.

"What the hell. Let's cut a rug."

And we are. Not only am I dancing with myself from a parallel universe, but our shoes are actually cutting the carpet beneath us. No, that's not good. Now I need to replace my rug.

"What the fuck, me! I didn't want us to actually destroy my carpet."

Wow, I really have got to take it easy on these pills. I wonder if this is a known side-effect.

"Oh, I do apologize for that, sir. You see, they've outlawed dance where I come from and now this might be my last chance. For once those pills wear off I'll be forced to return to my own dimension and live a life of boredom and silence."

"That really doesn't sound like it'd be too bad a place to call home. I've been looking for some peace and quiet myself. Any way I could swing by?"

"While that would be a most pleasant treat, sir, I don't think it'll be possible."

"I think I could pull it off. All I need to do is take a couple more pills and I should be all set. It's like I'll teleport there... Or something."

"I'm afraid I must advise against that, sir. I fear that if you were to take more you might not know where you are."

"Either way. Apparently, I'm a fantastic dancer."

"I will say, sir, I certainly have never been dipped this much before."

"You know you like it."

Yeah, he likes it.

"Quite."

"Yeah, that's it."

"Well, well. Look at the time, sir. I do say I must be going unfortunately. And you do look a bit tired from all the dancing and drugs, sir."

He's right. I'm fuckin' bushed!

"Until next time, me?"

"We'll see, sir. We'll see."

WHIP

Captain's log...

Ha! Log.

"So I've started self-medicating" I say to Henry, the vacuum.

He points his nozzle towards the floor. He clearly disapproves.

"Listen! It's obvious the pills aren't doing the trick. And I'm already on the maximum dosage. I needed to take situations into my own hands."

"But there are programs for this sort of thing," says the carpet sucker.

"Yeah, but not in this state. And fuck the man! I'm not paying taxes on this shit."

"We are aware of the fact that we're talking to a household appliance," says my brain, audibly.

"Yes, brain. We are aware of this."

I look down at the little bag containing my new "prescription."

"Hmm...," I say.

"A problem?" asks Henry.

"I think this batch is laced with something."

"How can you tell?" asks the inanimate object.

"You just answered your own question."

"How so?"

"You suck dirt! You shouldn't be able to talk. Let alone have a conversation with me."

"Na, see, I'm one of those new talking vacuums with a functioning brain and whatnot."

"Bull."

"No, totally. You just bought me the other day."

"Like fun I did. You're like six years old."

"And yesterday was my birthday!"

"You don't have one of those!"

"Are you saying I just magically appeared out of thin air? Do you know how re-goddamned-diculous that sounds?"

"As a matter of fact, I do. I'm talking to a FUCKING VACUUM!"

"Such childish behavior," says my brain, now floating around the room.

"Would you get back in my head!" I yell.

"Make me," it says.

"I'll show you who's a fucking vacuum," says Henry, raising his nozzle towards my mind.

"What are you doing?" I ask, knowing exactly what it is that bastard hoover is thinking.

"Hey, what are you doing?" asks my brain.

"Don't worry!" I shout over the loud sucking noise coming from Henry. My ass he's not a vacuum. I know a vacuum when I see one.

I run into the kitchen and swing open the refrigerator door. I don't know why I'm looking for a weapon in here, but I'm here now so I might as well look around.

I grab the whipped cream can and with what I could only assume is a mischievous glint in my eye I race back to the cleaning tool that's trying to devour my brain.

I pop the cap and bellow, "Take this, you... object!"

I press the button on the top of the canister and out shoots a cold stream of justice in the form of a whip. I snag Henry with my whipped cream whip and drag him closer to me. This is made exceedingly easy due the wheels Henry has screwed into his butt.

"If you haven't been sent here to clean up after me then why do you have this really long hose, wheels on your ass and are incredibly talented at sucking for hours on end."

Henry looks at me with his cold, lifeless attachments and says, "Because I'm a very generous and thoughtful lover."

I break the whip off the end of the canister, unclog my brain from the end of Henry's supposed mouth-tube or whatever and start spraying gallons of milky-white foam down his throat, I guess.

Henry collapses and spurts out some of the chilly dessert topping which magically floats away.

As my brain returns to my skull I look at the label of my trusty weapon.

"Huh. Didn't know that that's what they meant by 'Light.'"

ZEST

My doctor is going on about something. I should probably be paying attention to this. I'm sure it'll have something to do with my panic attacks. Damn things really toast my... buns? Eh, who knows.

"So you got all that?" he says.

"Yep."

He looks at me the way I look at peas. Or green beans. Or brussels sprouts. Or, well, pretty much any vegetable. He clearly knows I haven't been paying attention, but I just want to get out of here and back onto the couch with my good friends Bob, Sterling, Fry and Roger.

"And you'll let me know if you're hearing any more voices?" he says. "That's probably a sign that we need to adjust your medication."

"No problem," I say. And it wouldn't be, except for the fact that I kind of like them. They keep me company on those long winter nights in the fields. Hey, I'm just as confused as you are, but I feel good so fuck it. "Anything else I should know?"

"Just take it easy. Nothing too strenuous."

"I don't think that will be a problem. I just signed up to one of those streaming video services and I plan on getting my eight bucks worth and then some."

"Well you sound like you got things all figured out. I'd like to see you in a month to see how you're doing."

"And my friend wants to bang Kirsten Dunst, but I doubt Little Miss Chiclet-Teeth will be calling anytime soon."

"Pardon?"

"French?"

"You might want to get that prescription filled sooner rather than later. You're train-of-thought seems a bit..."

"Lemony?" I suggest.

"Sure, why not."

The pharmacy is packed. Just like my colon. I knew I should have stopped off at Burritos Burritos Burritos after coming here. But no! I had have six sopapillas.

I get on line and wait my turn. It's now a race between my ever-widening anus and the pharmacist. Just three people in front of me. I can do this. Wait! I forgot to factor in the time it'll take to talk to her. Plus the time to find a toilet afterwards. Shit. I think I may have to change my plans unless I want to change my pants. Not to mention the line forming behind me. Anxiety is like the worst thing for your bowels. Yeah. I'm going to have to make a break for it.

I dart from the line and make my way down a couple isles only knocking over three elderly women – A new record! – run out the exit and around to the back of the building. I drop my pants and proceed to fertilize the pavement.

"Nice butthole!" says a voice I hear coming from the wall behind me.

Marvelous! Either the store is talking to me or I'm hearing disembodied voices. I guess they both would be disembodied voices since stores don't have bodies. Well, they do in a ways. There's people in them and they have bodies. But what if they didn't? What if they just had heads with arms and legs flopping around? I have to remember to look that shit up on the internet when I get home.

"Hey!," says the strange voice.

"What?" I yell to no one in particular. Or the building itself. I don't know, I'm not well.

"Stop pooping on our wall!"

Holy crap on a biscotti, the store is sentient. I knew it!

"You have eyes?" I ask.

"There's a fucking camera looking right at you!" it says.

"Well aren't you saucy!"

"No, seriously! Stop taking a dump on the store!"

"Ugh! I hate it when stores refer to themselves in the third person."

"Listen, fucknuts! You're pooping on the store and we can see you thanks to the cameras we have set up in what we like to call the drive-thru prescription window."

Shit.

After a quick visit from the police, I'm on my way home with my medication. Thankfully I was just let off with a warning since this was my first offense and they took into account the massive amounts of Sertraline and Clonazepam I'm currently taking.

The good news is I'm fucking calm as shit now. You could smack me in the junk with a weed whacker a dozen or so times and I would not give a flying fuck. And speaking of weed, that helps too!

The bad news is I'm running out of food and in no way shape or form fit enough to leave... well this couch actually. I have the strangest feeling my motor skills might be

slightly impaired. But of all the bad news in the world, I'd say this is pretty low on the list.

BALANCE

There's a stillness in the air that whispers contentment. Every day should be like this day. My girlfriend and I are sitting on the couch reading a couple of books we picked up at the charity shop down the street. One of our cats in on my lap and the other is sitting between us. He's a fat little bastard so he likes his own cushion.

It's warm outside so our windows are open. It's surprisingly silent in the city. Everyone seems to be enjoying the rare blue sky and sun.

There's freshly-baked banana bread cooling on the counter. Dinner tonight is a margarita pizza from the Italian restaurant on the ground floor of our building. And for dessert? Stracciatella gelato.

I'm sufficiently medicated for all of today's activities. Which will essentially be books, food and television. I don't have to leave the house for anything until three days from now. And I most likely won't.

It already haunts me though. Every night, I lay awake dreading the impending doom up ahead. It rarely happens

right away. I'll usually just be there, trying to fall asleep and a random thought will slither into my head. It's most likely something about the future that could potentially happen. Or something in the distance that I know is there, but there are many ways for said situation to play out.

I'll try putting on my headphones and listening to some music. That's a tricky one too. Do I listen to something I know really well and risk my mind drifting and all of a sudden I'm in the midst of a full-blown panic attack without even realizing it? Or do I play something new that I don't know? If I do the latter I'll most likely be awake through the entire album because of how much attention I was giving each song; all the while not any closer to dreamland. Repeat ad infinitum.

Perhaps I'll get up and watch television, but again. The same concerns apply while adding to my sleep deprivation. Not to mention the crippling depression. Or the delusional behavior. Then the inevitable mood swing to hating just about everything and getting irritated by the most infinitesimal annoyance and not being able to do a single thing about anything. Then finally winding up in a fetal position on the floor as my limbs spasm out of control. I try to regain composure, but the only action I manage to muster is hitting myself or my surroundings as some form of distraction.

Eventually it subsides and I'm exhausted. Sleep comes almost immediately after laying back down in bed. It's reached the point where I almost expect this type of thing to happen every night. I'm so drained that I sleep most of the morning away, don't leave the house during the day and then have too much energy built up in me to sleep the next night. Everyone says to meditate or exercise, but those things just let the mind wander causing more trouble.

That is, unless I catch it in time and pop a pill to numb everything.

As far as I can tell there's no escape from the fear of the unknown. Except..., but even that has its own horror attached. The only way forward is to fight and hope that someday these feelings won't be a part of me anymore. Until then.

FRAY

Gotta get up for work. Gotta get up for work. Gotta get up for work. Gotta get up for work. Gotta get up for work. Gotta get up for work. Gotta get up for work. Gotta get up for work.

Really need to get up for work. Really need to get up for work. Really need to get up for work. Really need to get up for work. Really need to get up for work. Really need to get up for work. Really need to get up for work. Really need to get up for work. Really need to get up for work.

Shower time. Shower time. I can do this. Shower time. Shower time. I can totally do this. Shower time. A little shaky. Shower time.

"Hi penis!"

Brush the teeth. Brush the teeth. Easy. No problem. Shaking actually helps with this one. Don't throw up.

Put on work clothes. Put on work clothes. Put on work clothes. Too much. How about boxers? Put on boxers. Put on boxers. Put on boxers. Okay. Boxers are on. Socks. Putting on the socks. Socks go on feet. Feet meet socks.

Nervous tick. Right on schedule! Still making good time. Alright pants. I hate you. Pants on the legs. Putting on pants. Putting on pants. Not putting on pants. Sitting down. Going too fast. Ease into this.

Take two. Trying pants yet again. Legs go in the pants. One at a time. Pants go on legs. Friends. Pants. Pants. Pants are on. Belt! Where's that belt? Belt? The fuck, belt?

"Where's my goddamned fucking belt," I scream as I slam my fist into the wardrobe door. Clothing flies everywhere. My rage builds to a violent peak. I remember to breathe.

Late. Panic. Frantic text to manager. Feel the judgment through the phone. Find belt.

Buttoning up shirt. Buttoning up shirt. Buttoning up shirt. Cat hair everywhere. Lint roller under bed. Hand spazing out in an attempt to peel off dirty sheet. Roll myself up and down.

Walk into the kitchen. Grab a water. Take some pills. Walk out door. Walk out door. Walk out door. Walk out door. Walk out door. Punch door. Walk out door. Out of door. Lock apartment. Apartment locked.

Walking to work. Walking to work. Walking to work. People everywhere. They're all looking at me. Walking to work. No matter what street I take there's always someone there. Friends at work. Walk to friends. Walk to friends. Too crowded. Need to hide. Need to hide. Hiding. Hiding. People still walking passed. I can feel them spying on me.

"F-f-f-fuck. L-l-l-leave me a-a-a-lone!"

More people stare. Get to work. Safe at work. Get to work. Safe at work. Keep head down. Keep head down. Get to work. Safe.

Calming down. Friends are here. Taking another pill. Relax. Everything's okay. Just like every other day.

Shop's incredibly busy. There are customer's everywhere. One leaves two more come in. Absolute Hell. I'm here at the till just waiting for the next problem.

A gentleman approaches. The transaction is taking place. He's attempting to make small talk with me. I mess something up on the computer. I need to see his bank card again. He's not too happy.

"Why?" he asks.

"I did something out of order so I need to swipe it again." I respond truthfully.

"What did you fuck up?"

I love it when they curse at us.

"Uh," I start.

"You're not going to charge me twice, are you?"

"Of course not."

"If there's a second charge I'm going to come back in here and knock you the fuck out."

Jesus! I'm in my thirties and I still get talked to like this. The panic starts to set in again. My hands start shaking erratically. Co-workers come by to make sure I'm okay. I leave and head into the back office. Embarrassed beyond belief. Everyone saw that. Everyone thinks I'm a joke.

I'm told to go home. It's obvious that I'll be no help here. I begin my walk of shame back to my apartment. Everyone has to work harder now because of me. I fail them yet again.

WHIP

Do I go to the store?
Do I stay in?
Do I go to the store?
Do I stay in?
I technically have enough food to make it through the day. Of course some of that means eating expired milk in my cereal. I could skip the cereal and just have... Nothing as it would seem. Dry cereal works. And the marshmallow pieces are even better without milk. Especially rancid milk.

But if I went to the store I could get other things as well. Some type of sleep-aid would be nice. Or a shit-ton of alcohol would probably do the trick right about now. Maybe something to induce a carbohydrate coma. Pasta might do it. Or cookies! No, wait. Bagels. Toast a couple of those tasty bastards up, slather them with butter and watch the sheep come bounding over my bed.

That's it. I'm putting this to a vote. All those in favor of me going to the store and attempting to be a contributing

member of society, at least in an economic sense please say I.

"I," I say out-loud to reinforce the idea that this happened to be a good one.

All those opposed?

No.

That was odd.

"Is there someone else in here?"

I wait for the voice to come back, but there's just silence.

Fantastic. I thought this medication was supposed to stop me from being crazy. No, no. Get it out of your head. It was probably someone turning on their TV and not realizing that it was on super loud. That had to be it. Happy thoughts. I can do this.

I'm doing it. I'm walking to the store. Thankfully it's just a couple minutes down the road and not this epic quest. No thank you.

People pass by and I try to conceal my hands so my panic tremors don't show. It doesn't really work. I can tell that they see it. It's almost like I can hear their thoughts. They probably think I'm some raving drug addict coming off a bender. To be fair, I am on plenty of things that I probably could have a good time if things got desperate.

I reach the store and cautiously enter through the automatic doors. I really should have looked at the time before leaving because it seems like everyone is here getting their lunches. Plus there's a ton of teenagers. Is today a holiday or something? Fuck, I really didn't think this through all the way.

Nope.

Who the hell said that? I wasn't talking out-loud then was I? It's okay. Keep it together. Pick up a basket, get supplies and get the fuck out.

I start looking through the pre-made sandwiches, then the drinks, followed by the bakery.

Should probably pick up some fruit. Vitamins and stuff. I quickly turn back around to head towards the fresh fruit section when I accidentally bump into a very large man holding what I could only assume is the last bottle of olives. I assume this because of his reaction to me colliding into him, which is then immediately followed by him dropping the disgusting balls of ick and the glass bottle shattering as it hits the floor.

Plus the words he uses to describe my dumbassery really put the whole thing into perspective. But then, wouldn't you know it, that sets me off and I start shaking like a Torontonian prostitute in January. This leads me to knock into a couple other customers who also happen to be holding things that can break and they do.

Here I am, standing in the middle of the biggest clusterfuck since George W. Bush's brilliant idea to help the Iraqi citizens out by bombing the shit out of them, when the manager comes over. He sees me, spazing out like a meth addict watching Breaking Bad, and everyone else giving me nastier looks than the Smith family gave Miley.

And now I'm outside said store with more than just my ego bruised. Looks like it's dry cereal after all. Really rethinking taking this walk.

Told you.

FAINT

"I'll have the chicken and waffles!" I shout suddenly regaining consciousness.

I seem to be in a car of sort and holy shit! We're moving! Oh, no wait, I'm in the passenger seat. It appears they my girlfriend is driving. Thank some random deity for that.

"How long was I out," I ask her.

"About ten minutes. We were trying to figure out where to eat for lunch when you had another panic attack and passed the fuck out."

"Oh, did we decide on anywhere?"

"Nope."

"Sorry."

"It's okay. Not like you can help it. And besides, it's probably better to eat at your place anyway. Especially since we're dirt poor."

"Agreed."

We arrive at my apartment and it looks fabulous. Dirty dishes and cups litter every flat surface. Empty containers of food strewn across the floor.

"For fuck's sake! What the hell happened here?" my girlfriend asks with only the slightest hint of judgment.

"This? I haven't really been sleeping that much so I haven't really had the energy to clean, well, anything."

"The attacks getting that bad?"

"Yeah, I just start thinking whenever I try to fall asleep and then some silly thought will trigger it and then it's full swing."

"Has the depression at least gotten better?"

"Nope. It's all one giant circle of misery."

"That's awful."

"Fucking sucks a great big pulsating bag of dicks."

"That too."

"That's not all though."

She looks at me with this distressed look on her face. I know she really doesn't judge me. She's just concerned. Either that or she's really good at faking.

"What is it?" she asks bringing me back into the moment.

"I think the lack of sleep is causing me to hear voices."

"Oh."

Well, there's some judgment.

"They don't tell me to burn anything to try to assassinate a president to get some actress to notice me or anything like that. They're more like whispers. Hell, I guess it could all be the same voice or something. I don't know. I can't really make out any distinguishing factors."

Shit. Now she's crying.

"Hey, it's okay," I say, trying to reassure her. It's totally not working. I essentially told her I've just enrolled in the serial killer training program at Batshit University. Smooth!

"I know."

Holy crap! It worked!

"I know you're still you. And that it took a lot for you to tell me this."

"So you're not freaked out?"

"To be honest," she says as she takes my hand in hers, "I'm more scared than anything else. Have you thought of seeing anyone again or adjusting your medication?"

"Not really. I tend not to trust psychiatrists or therapists. I just don't feel comfortable talking with them. It's the whole judgment thing. I'm worried what they'll think of me."

"But it's their job. They've totally seen much crazier patients than you."

So now I'm crazy. Fan-fucking-tastic.

"You do have a point."

She actually does.

I know.

"Did you just hear that?" I ask her, hoping that she did. The walls are paper thin here so it's entirely possible to have been one of my neighbors.

"Hear what?" she says, visibly disturbed.

Balls!

Ask her to play with ours.

"That! Someone just asked you to play with my nuts. I heard it clear as day."

"Sorry. I wish I could say I did, but no. I'm sorry, sweetie."

"It's okay, I guess."

The fuck am I saying? I'm clearly hearing other voices in my head and they're me. This can't be good.

"I think you should make an appointment with someone. At least with your regular doctor."

"I'll call him in the morning."

"Thank you. Do you want me to stay the night?"

I should have her stay. Maybe the sex will be what I need to fall asleep. Afterwards that is.

No, sleep on her pillows!

Those aren't pillows!

They look soft enough to me.

On second thought...

On third thought, if you don't fuck her I will.

Yeah, I've lost it.

"I do want you to stay, but for reasons I'd really not like to get into right now I think it would be best for the three of us if you didn't sleep here tonight."

"The three of us?" she asks.

"Exactly."

RASH

Soul crushing darkness again, we see. Something different. We kid, we kid. Relax. Don't get worked up. We've come to expect this type of thing from ourselves. Lord knows we don't deal well with change.

Oh, don't bring God into this now. We thought we were going to make it all the way without.

It's a figure of speech.

We're a figure of speech.

Mature. Real mature.

Hey! We're the same person! There's no need for name calling.

Listen. We can't keep track of everyone inside this cluster-mind-fuck. We're seriously fucked up.

"Stop it!"

Like that's ever worked before. We're the one in control here.

What are we? Some alien goop that attached itsel—

You want to get sued? No, we're not... one of those.

Than what are we?

Fat.

Fuck us, buddy.

"Language."

Fuck off!

Good one.

Thanks.

Is it time for our life-altering speech yet?

What speech?

The one that leads to us never having to deal with any of this ever again.

We have a speech for that? What's it called?

Our momma.

Interesting title. Any seats left?

Haven't sold a single ticket yet. Which is a shame since it's a one-seat venue.

Is it? That's a little silly.

We know. Efficient: this place is not.

Where are we giving the speech?

Here.

No?

Yep.

Can we come?

Don't see why not. Hey, what do we know. The show's sold out now. We must have gotten the last seat.

What luck! Hold on...

Yeah...

Give us time. We know we're not all there.

We better. It's us for Christ's sake.

We thought we talked about this?

"Ugh"

We're cranky today.

"Please leave me alone."

But where would we go?

Yeah, there's not a lot of opportunities out there for us extra personalities. At least we can die with the notion that

we are probably the most insane person on the planet. We really should have had that tested before we hatched this plan.

What plan?

For fuck's sake, man! Are we really that dumb that we don't even know that we're going to be ending our own life.

Apparently, we're dumb as shit.

Whoa! Slow down there. Let's not give shit a bad name.

What did shit say?

How can poop talk?

We think we saw a documentary. Something about the holidays.

That was a cartoon.

We don't know. It was pretty graphic.

So, we doing this?

Maybe. Not really up to us. This is more of the body's forte.

Posh bastard.

We were wondering when we would show up.

We've been here the whole time.

We know. We saw us. We didn't feel like acknowledging us. Is that a crime?

We don't know. We don't make the laws here.

Yes. Yes we do.

Oh.

Speech?

We think the moment passed.

We do?

We do.

Do we?

Do we what?

Like dancing?

No, not really. Why?

No reason.

Because we stopped paying attention and now we don't know what to do next.

That usually is what happens.

Is it?

It is.

It is?

Tis.

Tits!

Where?!

Made us look! Oh!

Ha!

"GET OUT! GET OUT! GET OUT!"

Are we trying to pull eminent domain bullshit on ourselves. That's messed up.

Again, so are we.

Same here.

Ditto.

Ditto.

Ditto.

Ditto.

Ditto.

Ditto.

Ditto.

Ditto.

Ditto.

Ditto.

Did it just get darker? That's new.

Something new? Run away!

We're thoughts, idiot.

Hey, is the main guy here?

Like the first one? With the body?

Yeah, that shmuck.

Huh, no.

Shit.

Dependence

RASH

Soul crushing darkness again, we see. Something different. We kid, we kid. Relax. Don't get worked up. We've come to expect this type of thing from ourselves. Lord knows we don't deal well with change.

Oh, don't bring God into this now. We thought we were going to make it all the way without.

It's a figure of speech.

We're a figure of speech.

Mature. Real mature.

Hey! We're the same person! There's no need for name calling.

Listen. We can't keep track of everyone inside this cluster-mind-fuck. We're seriously fucked up.

"Stop it!"

Like that's ever worked before. We're the one in control here.

What are we? Some alien goop that attached itsel—

You want to get sued? No, we're not... one of those.

Than what are we?

Fat.

Fuck us, buddy.

"Language."

Fuck off!

Good one.

Thanks.

Is it time for our life-altering speech yet?

What speech?

The one that leads to us never having to deal with any of this ever again.

We have a speech for that? What's it called?

Our momma.

Interesting title. Any seats left?

Haven't sold a single ticket yet. Which is a shame since it's a one-seat venue.

Is it? That's a little silly.

We know. Efficient: this place is not.

Where are we giving the speech?

Here.

No?

Yep.

Can we come?

Don't see why not. Hey, what do we know. The show's sold out now. We must have gotten the last seat.

What luck! Hold on...

Yeah...

Give us time. We know we're not all there.

We better. It's us for Christ's sake.

We thought we talked about this?

"Ugh"

We're cranky today.

"Please leave me alone."

But where would we go?

Yeah, there's not a lot of opportunities out there for us extra personalities. At least we can die with the notion that

we are probably the most insane person on the planet. We really should have had that tested before we hatched this plan.

What plan?

For fuck's sake, man! Are we really that dumb that we don't even know that we're going to be ending our own life.

Apparently, we're dumb as shit.

Whoa! Slow down there. Let's not give shit a bad name.

What did shit say?

How can poop talk?

We think we saw a documentary. Something about the holidays.

That was a cartoon.

We don't know. It was pretty graphic.

So, we doing this?

Maybe. Not really up to us. This is more of the body's forte.

Posh bastard.

We were wondering when we would show up.

We've been here the whole time.

We know. We saw us. We didn't feel like acknowledging us. Is that a crime?

We don't know. We don't make the laws here.

Yes. Yes we do.

Oh.

Speech?

We think the moment passed.

We do?

We do.

Do we?

Do we what?

Like dancing?

No, not really. Why?

No reason.

Because we stopped paying attention and now we don't know what to do next.

That usually is what happens.

Is it?

It is.

It is?

Tis.

Tits!

Where?!

Made us look! Oh!

Ha!

"GET OUT! GET OUT! GET OUT!"

Are we trying to pull eminent domain bullshit on ourselves. That's messed up.

Again, so are we.

Same here.

Ditto.

Ditto.

Ditto.

Ditto.

Ditto.

Ditto.

Ditto.

Ditto.

Ditto.

Ditto.

Did it just get darker? That's new.

Something new? Run away!

We're thoughts, idiot.

Hey, is the main guy here?

Like the first one? With the body?

Yeah, that shmuck.

Huh, no.

Shit.

FAINT

"I'll have the chicken and waffles!" I shout suddenly regaining consciousness.

I seem to be in a car of sort and holy shit! We're moving! Oh, no wait, I'm in the passenger seat. It appears they my girlfriend is driving. Thank some random deity for that.

"How long was I out," I ask her.

"About ten minutes. We were trying to figure out where to eat for lunch when you had another panic attack and passed the fuck out."

"Oh, did we decide on anywhere?"

"Nope."

"Sorry."

"It's okay. Not like you can help it. And besides, it's probably better to eat at your place anyway. Especially since we're dirt poor."

"Agreed."

We arrive at my apartment and it looks fabulous. Dirty dishes and cups litter every flat surface. Empty containers of food strewn across the floor.

"For fuck's sake! What the hell happened here?" my girlfriend asks with only the slightest hint of judgment.

"This? I haven't really been sleeping that much so I haven't really had the energy to clean, well, anything."

"The attacks getting that bad?"

"Yeah, I just start thinking whenever I try to fall asleep and then some silly thought will trigger it and then it's full swing."

"Has the depression at least gotten better?"

"Nope. It's all one giant circle of misery."

"That's awful."

"Fucking sucks a great big pulsating bag of dicks."

"That too."

"That's not all though."

She looks at me with this distressed look on her face. I know she really doesn't judge me. She's just concerned. Either that or she's really good at faking.

"What is it?" she asks bringing me back into the moment.

"I think the lack of sleep is causing me to hear voices."

"Oh."

Well, there's some judgment.

"They don't tell me to burn anything to try to assassinate a president to get some actress to notice me or anything like that. They're more like whispers. Hell, I guess it could all be the same voice or something. I don't know. I can't really make out any distinguishing factors."

Shit. Now she's crying.

"Hey, it's okay," I say, trying to reassure her. It's totally not working. I essentially told her I've just enrolled in the serial killer training program at Batshit University. Smooth!

"I know."

Holy crap! It worked!

"I know you're still you. And that it took a lot for you to tell me this."

"So you're not freaked out?"

"To be honest," she says as she takes my hand in hers, "I'm more scared than anything else. Have you thought of seeing anyone again or adjusting your medication?"

"Not really. I tend not to trust psychiatrists or therapists. I just don't feel comfortable talking with them. It's the whole judgment thing. I'm worried what they'll think of me."

"But it's their job. They've totally seen much crazier patients than you."

So now I'm crazy. Fan-fucking-tastic.

"You do have a point."

She actually does.

I know.

"Did you just hear that?" I ask her, hoping that she did. The walls are paper thin here so it's entirely possible to have been one of my neighbors.

"Hear what?" she says, visibly disturbed.

Balls!

Ask her to play with ours.

"That! Someone just asked you to play with my nuts. I heard it clear as day."

"Sorry. I wish I could say I did, but no. I'm sorry, sweetie."

"It's okay, I guess."

The fuck am I saying? I'm clearly hearing other voices in my head and they're me. This can't be good.

"I think you should make an appointment with someone. At least with your regular doctor."

"I'll call him in the morning."

"Thank you. Do you want me to stay the night?"

I should have her stay. Maybe the sex will be what I need to fall asleep. Afterwards that is.

No, sleep on her pillows!

Those aren't pillows!

They look soft enough to me.

On second thought...

On third thought, if you don't fuck her I will.

Yeah, I've lost it.

"I do want you to stay, but for reasons I'd really not like to get into right now I think it would be best for the three of us if you didn't sleep here tonight."

"The three of us?" she asks.

"Exactly."

WHIP

Do I go to the store?
Do I stay in?
Do I go to the store?
Do I stay in?
I technically have enough food to make it through the day. Of course some of that means eating expired milk in my cereal. I could skip the cereal and just have... Nothing as it would seem. Dry cereal works. And the marshmallow pieces are even better without milk. Especially rancid milk.

But if I went to the store I could get other things as well. Some type of sleep-aid would be nice. Or a shit-ton of alcohol would probably do the trick right about now. Maybe something to induce a carbohydrate coma. Pasta might do it. Or cookies! No, wait. Bagels. Toast a couple of those tasty bastards up, slather them with butter and watch the sheep come bounding over my bed.

That's it. I'm putting this to a vote. All those in favor of me going to the store and attempting to be a contributing

member of society, at least in an economic sense please say I.

"I," I say out-loud to reinforce the idea that this happened to be a good one.

All those opposed?

No.

That was odd.

"Is there someone else in here?"

I wait for the voice to come back, but there's just silence.

Fantastic. I thought this medication was supposed to stop me from being crazy. No, no. Get it out of your head. It was probably someone turning on their TV and not realizing that it was on super loud. That had to be it. Happy thoughts. I can do this.

I'm doing it. I'm walking to the store. Thankfully it's just a couple minutes down the road and not this epic quest. No thank you.

People pass by and I try to conceal my hands so my panic tremors don't show. It doesn't really work. I can tell that they see it. It's almost like I can hear their thoughts. They probably think I'm some raving drug addict coming off a bender. To be fair, I am on plenty of things that I probably could have a good time if things got desperate.

I reach the store and cautiously enter through the automatic doors. I really should have looked at the time before leaving because it seems like everyone is here getting their lunches. Plus there's a ton of teenagers. Is today a holiday or something? Fuck, I really didn't think this through all the way.

Nope.

Who the hell said that? I wasn't talking out-loud then was I? It's okay. Keep it together. Pick up a basket, get supplies and get the fuck out.

I start looking through the pre-made sandwiches, then the drinks, followed by the bakery.

Should probably pick up some fruit. Vitamins and stuff. I quickly turn back around to head towards the fresh fruit section when I accidentally bump into a very large man holding what I could only assume is the last bottle of olives. I assume this because of his reaction to me colliding into him, which is then immediately followed by him dropping the disgusting balls of ick and the glass bottle shattering as it hits the floor.

Plus the words he uses to describe my dumbassery really put the whole thing into perspective. But then, wouldn't you know it, that sets me off and I start shaking like a Torontonian prostitute in January. This leads me to knock into a couple other customers who also happen to be holding things that can break and they do.

Here I am, standing in the middle of the biggest clusterfuck since George W. Bush's brilliant idea to help the Iraqi citizens out by bombing the shit out of them, when the manager comes over. He sees me, spazing out like a meth addict watching Breaking Bad, and everyone else giving me nastier looks than the Smith family gave Miley.

And now I'm outside said store with more than just my ego bruised. Looks like it's dry cereal after all. Really rethinking taking this walk.

Told you.

FRAY

Gotta get up for work. Gotta get up for work. Gotta get up for work. Gotta get up for work. Gotta get up for work. Gotta get up for work. Gotta get up for work. Gotta get up for work.

Really need to get up for work. Really need to get up for work. Really need to get up for work. Really need to get up for work. Really need to get up for work. Really need to get up for work. Really need to get up for work. Really need to get up for work. Really need to get up for work.

Shower time. Shower time. I can do this. Shower time. Shower time. I can totally do this. Shower time. A little shaky. Shower time.

"Hi penis!"

Brush the teeth. Brush the teeth. Easy. No problem. Shaking actually helps with this one. Don't throw up.

Put on work clothes. Put on work clothes. Put on work clothes. Too much. How about boxers? Put on boxers. Put on boxers. Put on boxers. Okay. Boxers are on. Socks. Putting on the socks. Socks go on feet. Feet meet socks.

Nervous tick. Right on schedule! Still making good time. Alright pants. I hate you. Pants on the legs. Putting on pants. Putting on pants. Not putting on pants. Sitting down. Going too fast. Ease into this.

Take two. Trying pants yet again. Legs go in the pants. One at a time. Pants go on legs. Friends. Pants. Pants. Pants are on. Belt! Where's that belt? Belt? The fuck, belt?

"Where's my goddamned fucking belt," I scream as I slam my fist into the wardrobe door. Clothing flies everywhere. My rage builds to a violent peak. I remember to breathe.

Late. Panic. Frantic text to manager. Feel the judgment through the phone. Find belt.

Buttoning up shirt. Buttoning up shirt. Buttoning up shirt. Cat hair everywhere. Lint roller under bed. Hand spazing out in an attempt to peel off dirty sheet. Roll myself up and down.

Walk into the kitchen. Grab a water. Take some pills. Walk out door. Walk out door. Walk out door. Walk out door. Walk out door. Punch door. Walk out door. Out of door. Lock apartment. Apartment locked.

Walking to work. Walking to work. Walking to work. People everywhere. They're all looking at me. Walking to work. No matter what street I take there's always someone there. Friends at work. Walk to friends. Walk to friends. Too crowded. Need to hide. Need to hide. Hiding. Hiding. People still walking passed. I can feel them spying on me.

"F-f-f-fuck. L-l-l-leave me a-a-a-lone!"

More people stare. Get to work. Safe at work. Get to work. Safe at work. Keep head down. Keep head down. Get to work. Safe.

Calming down. Friends are here. Taking another pill. Relax. Everything's okay. Just like every other day.

Shop's incredibly busy. There are customer's everywhere. One leaves two more come in. Absolute Hell. I'm here at the till just waiting for the next problem.

A gentleman approaches. The transaction is taking place. He's attempting to make small talk with me. I mess something up on the computer. I need to see his bank card again. He's not too happy.

"Why?" he asks.

"I did something out of order so I need to swipe it again." I respond truthfully.

"What did you fuck up?"

I love it when they curse at us.

"Uh," I start.

"You're not going to charge me twice, are you?"

"Of course not."

"If there's a second charge I'm going to come back in here and knock you the fuck out."

Jesus! I'm in my thirties and I still get talked to like this. The panic starts to set in again. My hands start shaking erratically. Co-workers come by to make sure I'm okay. I leave and head into the back office. Embarrassed beyond belief. Everyone saw that. Everyone thinks I'm a joke.

I'm told to go home. It's obvious that I'll be no help here. I begin my walk of shame back to my apartment. Everyone has to work harder now because of me. I fail them yet again.

BALANCE

There's a stillness in the air that whispers contentment. Every day should be like this day. My girlfriend and I are sitting on the couch reading a couple of books we picked up at the charity shop down the street. One of our cats in on my lap and the other is sitting between us. He's a fat little bastard so he likes his own cushion.

It's warm outside so our windows are open. It's surprisingly silent in the city. Everyone seems to be enjoying the rare blue sky and sun.

There's freshly-baked banana bread cooling on the counter. Dinner tonight is a margarita pizza from the Italian restaurant on the ground floor of our building. And for dessert? Stracciatella gelato.

I'm sufficiently medicated for all of today's activities. Which will essentially be books, food and television. I don't have to leave the house for anything until three days from now. And I most likely won't.

It already haunts me though. Every night, I lay awake dreading the impending doom up ahead. It rarely happens

right away. I'll usually just be there, trying to fall asleep and a random thought will slither into my head. It's most likely something about the future that could potentially happen. Or something in the distance that I know is there, but there are many ways for said situation to play out.

I'll try putting on my headphones and listening to some music. That's a tricky one too. Do I listen to something I know really well and risk my mind drifting and all of a sudden I'm in the midst of a full-blown panic attack without even realizing it? Or do I play something new that I don't know? If I do the latter I'll most likely be awake through the entire album because of how much attention I was giving each song; all the while not any closer to dreamland. Repeat ad infinitum.

Perhaps I'll get up and watch television, but again. The same concerns apply while adding to my sleep deprivation. Not to mention the crippling depression. Or the delusional behavior. Then the inevitable mood swing to hating just about everything and getting irritated by the most infinitesimal annoyance and not being able to do a single thing about anything. Then finally winding up in a fetal position on the floor as my limbs spasm out of control. I try to regain composure, but the only action I manage to muster is hitting myself or my surroundings as some form of distraction.

Eventually it subsides and I'm exhausted. Sleep comes almost immediately after laying back down in bed. It's reached the point where I almost expect this type of thing to happen every night. I'm so drained that I sleep most of the morning away, don't leave the house during the day and then have too much energy built up in me to sleep the next night. Everyone says to meditate or exercise, but those things just let the mind wander causing more trouble.

That is, unless I catch it in time and pop a pill to numb everything.

As far as I can tell there's no escape from the fear of the unknown. Except..., but even that has its own horror attached. The only way forward is to fight and hope that someday these feelings won't be a part of me anymore. Until then.

ZEST

My doctor is going on about something. I should probably be paying attention to this. I'm sure it'll have something to do with my panic attacks. Damn things really toast my... buns? Eh, who knows.

"So you got all that?" he says.

"Yep."

He looks at me the way I look at peas. Or green beans. Or brussels sprouts. Or, well, pretty much any vegetable. He clearly knows I haven't been paying attention, but I just want to get out of here and back onto the couch with my good friends Bob, Sterling, Fry and Roger.

"And you'll let me know if you're hearing any more voices?" he says. "That's probably a sign that we need to adjust your medication."

"No problem," I say. And it wouldn't be, except for the fact that I kind of like them. They keep me company on those long winter nights in the fields. Hey, I'm just as confused as you are, but I feel good so fuck it. "Anything else I should know?"

"Just take it easy. Nothing too strenuous."

"I don't think that will be a problem. I just signed up to one of those streaming video services and I plan on getting my eight bucks worth and then some."

"Well you sound like you got things all figured out. I'd like to see you in a month to see how you're doing."

"And my friend wants to bang Kirsten Dunst, but I doubt Little Miss Chiclet-Teeth will be calling anytime soon."

"Pardon?"

"French?"

"You might want to get that prescription filled sooner rather than later. You're train-of-thought seems a bit..."

"Lemony?" I suggest.

"Sure, why not."

The pharmacy is packed. Just like my colon. I knew I should have stopped off at Burritos Burritos Burritos after coming here. But no! I had have six sopapillas.

I get on line and wait my turn. It's now a race between my ever-widening anus and the pharmacist. Just three people in front of me. I can do this. Wait! I forgot to factor in the time it'll take to talk to her. Plus the time to find a toilet afterwards. Shit. I think I may have to change my plans unless I want to change my pants. Not to mention the line forming behind me. Anxiety is like the worst thing for your bowels. Yeah. I'm going to have to make a break for it.

I dart from the line and make my way down a couple isles only knocking over three elderly women – A new record! – run out the exit and around to the back of the building. I drop my pants and proceed to fertilize the pavement.

"Nice butthole!" says a voice I hear coming from the wall behind me.

Marvelous! Either the store is talking to me or I'm hearing disembodied voices. I guess they both would be disembodied voices since stores don't have bodies. Well, they do in a ways. There's people in them and they have bodies. But what if they didn't? What if they just had heads with arms and legs flopping around? I have to remember to look that shit up on the internet when I get home.

"Hey!," says the strange voice.

"What?" I yell to no one in particular. Or the building itself. I don't know, I'm not well.

"Stop pooping on our wall!"

Holy crap on a biscotti, the store is sentient. I knew it!

"You have eyes?" I ask.

"There's a fucking camera looking right at you!" it says.

"Well aren't you saucy!"

"No, seriously! Stop taking a dump on the store!"

"Ugh! I hate it when stores refer to themselves in the third person."

"Listen, fucknuts! You're pooping on the store and we can see you thanks to the cameras we have set up in what we like to call the drive-thru prescription window."

Shit.

After a quick visit from the police, I'm on my way home with my medication. Thankfully I was just let off with a warning since this was my first offense and they took into account the massive amounts of Sertraline and Clonazepam I'm currently taking.

The good news is I'm fucking calm as shit now. You could smack me in the junk with a weed whacker a dozen or so times and I would not give a flying fuck. And speaking of weed, that helps too!

The bad news is I'm running out of food and in no way shape or form fit enough to leave... well this couch actually. I have the strangest feeling my motor skills might be

slightly impaired. But of all the bad news in the world, I'd say this is pretty low on the list.

WHIP

Captain's log...

Ha! Log.

"So I've started self-medicating" I say to Henry, the vacuum.

He points his nozzle towards the floor. He clearly disapproves.

"Listen! It's obvious the pills aren't doing the trick. And I'm already on the maximum dosage. I needed to take situations into my own hands."

"But there are programs for this sort of thing," says the carpet sucker.

"Yeah, but not in this state. And fuck the man! I'm not paying taxes on this shit."

"We are aware of the fact that we're talking to a household appliance," says my brain, audibly.

"Yes, brain. We are aware of this."

I look down at the little bag containing my new "prescription."

"Hmm...," I say.

"A problem?" asks Henry.

"I think this batch is laced with something."

"How can you tell?" asks the inanimate object.

"You just answered your own question."

"How so?"

"You suck dirt! You shouldn't be able to talk. Let alone have a conversation with me."

"Na, see, I'm one of those new talking vacuums with a functioning brain and whatnot."

"Bull."

"No, totally. You just bought me the other day."

"Like fun I did. You're like six years old."

"And yesterday was my birthday!"

"You don't have one of those!"

"Are you saying I just magically appeared out of thin air? Do you know how re-goddamned-diculous that sounds?"

"As a matter of fact, I do. I'm talking to a FUCKING VACUUM!"

"Such childish behavior," says my brain, now floating around the room.

"Would you get back in my head!" I yell.

"Make me," it says.

"I'll show you who's a fucking vacuum," says Henry, raising his nozzle towards my mind.

"What are you doing?" I ask, knowing exactly what it is that bastard hoover is thinking.

"Hey, what are you doing?" asks my brain.

"Don't worry!" I shout over the loud sucking noise coming from Henry. My ass he's not a vacuum. I know a vacuum when I see one.

I run into the kitchen and swing open the refrigerator door. I don't know why I'm looking for a weapon in here, but I'm here now so I might as well look around.

I grab the whipped cream can and with what I could only assume is a mischievous glint in my eye I race back to the cleaning tool that's trying to devour my brain.

I pop the cap and bellow, "Take this, you... object!"

I press the button on the top of the canister and out shoots a cold stream of justice in the form of a whip. I snag Henry with my whipped cream whip and drag him closer to me. This is made exceedingly easy due the wheels Henry has screwed into his butt.

"If you haven't been sent here to clean up after me then why do you have this really long hose, wheels on your ass and are incredibly talented at sucking for hours on end."

Henry looks at me with his cold, lifeless attachments and says, "Because I'm a very generous and thoughtful lover."

I break the whip off the end of the canister, unclog my brain from the end of Henry's supposed mouth-tube or whatever and start spraying gallons of milky-white foam down his throat, I guess.

Henry collapses and spurts out some of the chilly dessert topping which magically floats away.

As my brain returns to my skull I look at the label of my trusty weapon.

"Huh. Didn't know that that's what they meant by 'Light.'"

REEL

Morning again! Awesome! Another day where I don't get to go anywhere because they're out there. With their prying eyes and judgmental... brains! For the love of... What the Hell is wrong with me?

"I can help you with that question," says a voice that I'm not one hundred percent sure is actually real.

"And who might you be?" I ask, actually expecting a response.

"I am you..."

Great.

"From a different dimension," the voice continues.

"I see. You wouldn't have anything to do with the insanely large vat of anxiety pills I took before, would you?"

"Perhaps."

"Right. So, if you don't mind. I'd like to go about my day. I have a busy schedule of watching cartoons and glaring out the window at all of the well-adjusted people going about their normal lives and so forth. You know. Work and shit."

"I'm sorry, sir. I didn't know you had so much on your plate," says the voice while finally taking the physical form of me, but dressed in a top hat and tails.

"Holy fuck," I literally say to myself. "Even I want to whack myself in the nuts. Why the hell am I dressed like that?"

"Just thought it was the thing to do," said my other-worldly self, almost imitating Jacob Marley's inflection from one of the televised Dickens productions.

"Uh huh."

"Care to dance, sir?"

"Why are you calling me 'sir?' We're the same person. I shouldn't be a higher class than you. For fuck's sake man, I'm stoned out of my gourd. Wait. Did you just ask me to dance?"

"Indeed I did, sir. Around the fountain, perchance?"

Well I'll be a... robot's antenna, I don't know. My bedroom now has a fountain in the middle of it. Not to mention the four-piece string section that magically appeared out of nowhere.

"What the hell. Let's cut a rug."

And we are. Not only am I dancing with myself from a parallel universe, but our shoes are actually cutting the carpet beneath us. No, that's not good. Now I need to replace my rug.

"What the fuck, me! I didn't want us to actually destroy my carpet."

Wow, I really have got to take it easy on these pills. I wonder if this is a known side-effect.

"Oh, I do apologize for that, sir. You see, they've outlawed dance where I come from and now this might be my last chance. For once those pills wear off I'll be forced to return to my own dimension and live a life of boredom and silence."

"That really doesn't sound like it'd be too bad a place to call home. I've been looking for some peace and quiet myself. Any way I could swing by?"

"While that would be a most pleasant treat, sir, I don't think it'll be possible."

"I think I could pull it off. All I need to do is take a couple more pills and I should be all set. It's like I'll teleport there... Or something."

"I'm afraid I must advise against that, sir. I fear that if you were to take more you might not know where you are."

"Either way. Apparently, I'm a fantastic dancer."

"I will say, sir, I certainly have never been dipped this much before."

"You know you like it."

Yeah, he likes it.

"Quite."

"Yeah, that's it."

"Well, well. Look at the time, sir. I do say I must be going unfortunately. And you do look a bit tired from all the dancing and drugs, sir."

He's right. I'm fuckin' bushed!

"Until next time, me?"

"We'll see, sir. We'll see."

RECESS

Complete darkness. Ah, just me and my thoughts. That is until that blasted sun shows up and takes a bright luminescent shit on everything. And here he comes now.

I'm standing on some sort of mountain watching some kind of creature flying around some point in the distance. I patiently wait for my chance to strike because that's what you do in these situations. Right? I hear its shrill screech as it starts to become clearer. I leap into action.

I misjudge the jump and miss the creature completely. During the fall I manage to turn myself around and finally get a decent look at the flying abomination I've been tussling with up here on the cloud-engulfed rock.

"A fucking dragon?" I say, still falling to my imminent death. "Nope! I'm out."

"Grrrowl?" asks the dragon as it dives after me.

"Back, you flying lizard!"

"Hey there, hold on a second" it says. "You can't use the L word! That's our word."

"Shit, sorry," I say, "I had no idea. I meant no disrespect by it."

It replies, "While I believe that you were not aware of its derogatory nature making this all a silly little coincident, but I will have to beg to differ with you, my good man."

"Huh?"

"You see," the dragon continues, "while you didn't know you weren't a'supposed to say that word, ya did mean some disrespect."

One doesn't normally see a dragon turn into a little gumdrop pony, but there it is. Right in front of me. At this very minute. Man, I wish I had a camera.

"Hey!" squeaks the adorable, yet edible, gummy pony prancing about my feet. "We were having a conversation, Mister-I-don't-give-two-shits-about-what-you're-saying-so-I'm-going-to-look-off-in-the-distance-with-the-dumbest-look-on-my-face—"

"I guess I did kind of space out there for a mini—"

"And now you're interrupting me too! I should smite you down to the depths of Hell to pathetic little imp. I'll grind your bones to dust and sprinkle them on top of just some of the most diabetes-inducing cupcakes your twinkling peepers ever did see, Fuckface."

Okay. I'm frozen in terror and pee. Mostly pee.

"What just happened there?" I ask.

"Oh, that," says the I-don't-know-what. "I change shape randomly. Major fuckin' ball ache, let me tell you!"

"So what are you supposed to be now?"

"Fuck if I know. This is your brain after all. As far as I can tell you either took a LOT of hallucinogens or..."

"Or what?"

"Or you're really fucked up in the head."

"Oh, it's the latter."

"Ya think?"

"Oh totally. I stopped taking acid like weeks ago."

"Fantastic!" said the anthropomorphized bicycle hovering in front of me. "Also, why do I have the urge to ask you to hop on me and move your feet around?"

"You're a bike."

"I see."

"You're hovering though, that's cool.

The bike released some tire pressure.

"Did you just fart?"

"I think I did."

Now it's a flying bookcase with every Science Fiction book ever written on it.

"So... Now you're a bookcase," I pronounce astutely.

"Not just any bookcase," says the furniture using a voice that brings to mind images of ghosts and goblins, "but a magic Sci-Fi one! I'm going to go off and read a few of these before I turn into the Queen of England's vibrator. Oh, how terrifying."

It's flying away now. Come to think of it, I'm flying as well. Wasn't I falling a little while ago? Where the fuck am I?

I land safely on the floor that just happen to appear from out of thin air and can't seem to find anyone who might know what's happening.

I hear a voice slither into my ear and say, "What about that bookcase dude? He was pretty cool."

"I looked, but I can't even find him now."

A slight buzzing rolls in from off in the distance. A couch appears. A woman of considerable age is facing the opposite direction. The buzzing suddenly stops. She rests her head back.

As I, quite rapidly, adjust my position from vertical to something more horizontal, a flick of what must be a lighter shatters the silence. As the darkness slowly creeps in, the faintest trail of smoke rises above her crown.

Desire

RECESS

Complete darkness. Ah, just me and my thoughts. That is until that blasted sun shows up and takes a bright luminescent shit on everything. And here he comes now.

I'm standing on some sort of mountain watching some kind of creature flying around some point in the distance. I patiently wait for my chance to strike because that's what you do in these situations. Right? I hear its shrill screech as it starts to become clearer. I leap into action.

I misjudge the jump and miss the creature completely. During the fall I manage to turn myself around and finally get a decent look at the flying abomination I've been tussling with up here on the cloud-engulfed rock.

"A fucking dragon?" I say, still falling to my imminent death. "Nope! I'm out."

"Grrrowl?" asks the dragon as it dives after me.

"Back, you flying lizard!"

"Hey there, hold on a second" it says. "You can't use the L word! That's our word."

"Shit, sorry," I say, "I had no idea. I meant no disrespect by it."

It replies, "While I believe that you were not aware of its derogatory nature making this all a silly little coincident, but I will have to beg to differ with you, my good man."

"Huh?"

"You see," the dragon continues, "while you didn't know you weren't a'supposed to say that word, ya did mean some disrespect."

One doesn't normally see a dragon turn into a little gumdrop pony, but there it is. Right in front of me. At this very minute. Man, I wish I had a camera.

"Hey!" squeaks the adorable, yet edible, gummy pony prancing about my feet. "We were having a conversation, Mister-I-don't-give-two-shits-about-what-you're-saying-so-I'm-going-to-look-off-in-the-distance-with-the-dumbest-look-on-my-face—"

"I guess I did kind of space out there for a mini—"

"And now you're interrupting me too! I should smite you down to the depths of Hell to pathetic little imp. I'll grind your bones to dust and sprinkle them on top of just some of the most diabetes-inducing cupcakes your twinkling peepers ever did see, Fuckface."

Okay. I'm frozen in terror and pee. Mostly pee.

"What just happened there?" I ask.

"Oh, that," says the I-don't-know-what. "I change shape randomly. Major fuckin' ball ache, let me tell you!"

"So what are you supposed to be now?"

"Fuck if I know. This is your brain after all. As far as I can tell you either took a LOT of hallucinogens or..."

"Or what?"

"Or you're really fucked up in the head."

"Oh, it's the latter."

"Ya think?"

"Oh totally. I stopped taking acid like weeks ago."

"Fantastic!" said the anthropomorphized bicycle hovering in front of me. "Also, why do I have the urge to ask you to hop on me and move your feet around?"

"You're a bike."

"I see."

"You're hovering though, that's cool.

The bike released some tire pressure.

"Did you just fart?"

"I think I did."

Now it's a flying bookcase with every Science Fiction book ever written on it.

"So... Now you're a bookcase," I pronounce astutely.

"Not just any bookcase," says the furniture using a voice that brings to mind images of ghosts and goblins, "but a magic Sci-Fi one! I'm going to go off and read a few of these before I turn into the Queen of England's vibrator. Oh, how terrifying."

It's flying away now. Come to think of it, I'm flying as well. Wasn't I falling a little while ago? Where the fuck am I?

I land safely on the floor that just happen to appear from out of thin air and can't seem to find anyone who might know what's happening.

I hear a voice slither into my ear and say, "What about that bookcase dude? He was pretty cool."

"I looked, but I can't even find him now."

A slight buzzing rolls in from off in the distance. A couch appears. A woman of considerable age is facing the opposite direction. The buzzing suddenly stops. She rests her head back.

As I, quite rapidly, adjust my position from vertical to something more horizontal, a flick of what must be a lighter shatters the silence. As the darkness slowly creeps in, the faintest trail of smoke rises above her crown.

RASH

Soul crushing darkness again, we see. Something different. We kid, we kid. Relax. Don't get worked up. We've come to expect this type of thing from ourselves. Lord knows we don't deal well with change.

Oh, don't bring God into this now. We thought we were going to make it all the way without.

It's a figure of speech.

We're a figure of speech.

Mature. Real mature.

Hey! We're the same person! There's no need for name calling.

Listen. We can't keep track of everyone inside this cluster-mind-fuck. We're seriously fucked up.

"Stop it!"

Like that's ever worked before. We're the one in control here.

What are we? Some alien goop that attached itsel—

You want to get sued? No, we're not... one of those.

Than what are we?

Fat.

Fuck us, buddy.

"Language."

Fuck off!

Good one.

Thanks.

Is it time for our life-altering speech yet?

What speech?

The one that leads to us never having to deal with any of this ever again.

We have a speech for that? What's it called?

Our momma.

Interesting title. Any seats left?

Haven't sold a single ticket yet. Which is a shame since it's a one-seat venue.

Is it? That's a little silly.

We know. Efficient: this place is not.

Where are we giving the speech?

Here.

No?

Yep.

Can we come?

Don't see why not. Hey, what do we know. The show's sold out now. We must have gotten the last seat.

What luck! Hold on...

Yeah...

Give us time. We know we're not all there.

We better. It's us for Christ's sake.

We thought we talked about this?

"Ugh"

We're cranky today.

"Please leave me alone."

But where would we go?

Yeah, there's not a lot of opportunities out there for us extra personalities. At least we can die with the notion that

we are probably the most insane person on the planet. We really should have had that tested before we hatched this plan.

What plan?

For fuck's sake, man! Are we really that dumb that we don't even know that we're going to be ending our own life.

Apparently, we're dumb as shit.

Whoa! Slow down there. Let's not give shit a bad name.

What did shit say?

How can poop talk?

We think we saw a documentary. Something about the holidays.

That was a cartoon.

We don't know. It was pretty graphic.

So, we doing this?

Maybe. Not really up to us. This is more of the body's forte.

Posh bastard.

We were wondering when we would show up.

We've been here the whole time.

We know. We saw us. We didn't feel like acknowledging us. Is that a crime?

We don't know. We don't make the laws here.

Yes. Yes we do.

Oh.

Speech?

We think the moment passed.

We do?

We do.

Do we?

Do we what?

Like dancing?

No, not really. Why?

No reason.

Because we stopped paying attention and now we don't know what to do next.

That usually is what happens.

Is it?

It is.

It is?

Tis.

Tits!

Where?!

Made us look! Oh!

Ha!

"GET OUT! GET OUT! GET OUT!"

Are we trying to pull eminent domain bullshit on ourselves. That's messed up.

Again, so are we.

Same here.

Ditto.

Ditto.

Ditto.

Ditto.

Ditto.

Ditto.

Ditto.

Ditto.

Ditto.

Ditto.

Did it just get darker? That's new.

Something new? Run away!

We're thoughts, idiot.

Hey, is the main guy here?

Like the first one? With the body?

Yeah, that shmuck.

Huh, no.

Shit.

REEL

Morning again! Awesome! Another day where I don't get to go anywhere because they're out there. With their prying eyes and judgmental... brains! For the love of... What the Hell is wrong with me?

"I can help you with that question," says a voice that I'm not one hundred percent sure is actually real.

"And who might you be?" I ask, actually expecting a response.

"I am you..."

Great.

"From a different dimension," the voice continues.

"I see. You wouldn't have anything to do with the insanely large vat of anxiety pills I took before, would you?"

"Perhaps."

"Right. So, if you don't mind. I'd like to go about my day. I have a busy schedule of watching cartoons and glaring out the window at all of the well-adjusted people going about their normal lives and so forth. You know. Work and shit."

"I'm sorry, sir. I didn't know you had so much on your plate," says the voice while finally taking the physical form of me, but dressed in a top hat and tails.

"Holy fuck," I literally say to myself. "Even I want to whack myself in the nuts. Why the hell am I dressed like that?"

"Just thought it was the thing to do," said my other-worldly self, almost imitating Jacob Marley's inflection from one of the televised Dickens productions.

"Uh huh."

"Care to dance, sir?"

"Why are you calling me 'sir?' We're the same person. I shouldn't be a higher class than you. For fuck's sake man, I'm stoned out of my gourd. Wait. Did you just ask me to dance?"

"Indeed I did, sir. Around the fountain, perchance?"

Well I'll be a... robot's antenna, I don't know. My bedroom now has a fountain in the middle of it. Not to mention the four-piece string section that magically appeared out of nowhere.

"What the hell. Let's cut a rug."

And we are. Not only am I dancing with myself from a parallel universe, but our shoes are actually cutting the carpet beneath us. No, that's not good. Now I need to replace my rug.

"What the fuck, me! I didn't want us to actually destroy my carpet."

Wow, I really have got to take it easy on these pills. I wonder if this is a known side-effect.

"Oh, I do apologize for that, sir. You see, they've outlawed dance where I come from and now this might be my last chance. For once those pills wear off I'll be forced to return to my own dimension and live a life of boredom and silence."

"That really doesn't sound like it'd be too bad a place to call home. I've been looking for some peace and quiet myself. Any way I could swing by?"

"While that would be a most pleasant treat, sir, I don't think it'll be possible."

"I think I could pull it off. All I need to do is take a couple more pills and I should be all set. It's like I'll teleport there... Or something."

"I'm afraid I must advise against that, sir. I fear that if you were to take more you might not know where you are."

"Either way. Apparently, I'm a fantastic dancer."

"I will say, sir, I certainly have never been dipped this much before."

"You know you like it."

Yeah, he likes it.

"Quite."

"Yeah, that's it."

"Well, well. Look at the time, sir. I do say I must be going unfortunately. And you do look a bit tired from all the dancing and drugs, sir."

He's right. I'm fuckin' bushed!

"Until next time, me?"

"We'll see, sir. We'll see."

FAINT

"I'll have the chicken and waffles!" I shout suddenly regaining consciousness.

I seem to be in a car of sort and holy shit! We're moving! Oh, no wait, I'm in the passenger seat. It appears they my girlfriend is driving. Thank some random deity for that.

"How long was I out," I ask her.

"About ten minutes. We were trying to figure out where to eat for lunch when you had another panic attack and passed the fuck out."

"Oh, did we decide on anywhere?"

"Nope."

"Sorry."

"It's okay. Not like you can help it. And besides, it's probably better to eat at your place anyway. Especially since we're dirt poor."

"Agreed."

We arrive at my apartment and it looks fabulous. Dirty dishes and cups litter every flat surface. Empty containers of food strewn across the floor.

"For fuck's sake! What the hell happened here?" my girlfriend asks with only the slightest hint of judgment.

"This? I haven't really been sleeping that much so I haven't really had the energy to clean, well, anything."

"The attacks getting that bad?"

"Yeah, I just start thinking whenever I try to fall asleep and then some silly thought will trigger it and then it's full swing."

"Has the depression at least gotten better?"

"Nope. It's all one giant circle of misery."

"That's awful."

"Fucking sucks a great big pulsating bag of dicks."

"That too."

"That's not all though."

She looks at me with this distressed look on her face. I know she really doesn't judge me. She's just concerned. Either that or she's really good at faking.

"What is it?" she asks bringing me back into the moment.

"I think the lack of sleep is causing me to hear voices."

"Oh."

Well, there's some judgment.

"They don't tell me to burn anything to try to assassinate a president to get some actress to notice me or anything like that. They're more like whispers. Hell, I guess it could all be the same voice or something. I don't know. I can't really make out any distinguishing factors."

Shit. Now she's crying.

"Hey, it's okay," I say, trying to reassure her. It's totally not working. I essentially told her I've just enrolled in the serial killer training program at Batshit University. Smooth!

"I know."

Holy crap! It worked!

"I know you're still you. And that it took a lot for you to tell me this."

"So you're not freaked out?"

"To be honest," she says as she takes my hand in hers, "I'm more scared than anything else. Have you thought of seeing anyone again or adjusting your medication?"

"Not really. I tend not to trust psychiatrists or therapists. I just don't feel comfortable talking with them. It's the whole judgment thing. I'm worried what they'll think of me."

"But it's their job. They've totally seen much crazier patients than you."

So now I'm crazy. Fan-fucking-tastic.

"You do have a point."

She actually does.

I know.

"Did you just hear that?" I ask her, hoping that she did. The walls are paper thin here so it's entirely possible to have been one of my neighbors.

"Hear what?" she says, visibly disturbed.

Balls!

Ask her to play with ours.

"That! Someone just asked you to play with my nuts. I heard it clear as day."

"Sorry. I wish I could say I did, but no. I'm sorry, sweetie."

"It's okay, I guess."

The fuck am I saying? I'm clearly hearing other voices in my head and they're me. This can't be good.

"I think you should make an appointment with someone. At least with your regular doctor."

"I'll call him in the morning."

"Thank you. Do you want me to stay the night?"

I should have her stay. Maybe the sex will be what I need to fall asleep. Afterwards that is.

No, sleep on her pillows!

Those aren't pillows!

They look soft enough to me.

On second thought...

On third thought, if you don't fuck her I will.

Yeah, I've lost it.

"I do want you to stay, but for reasons I'd really not like to get into right now I think it would be best for the three of us if you didn't sleep here tonight."

"The three of us?" she asks.

"Exactly."

WHIP

Captain's log...

Ha! Log.

"So I've started self-medicating" I say to Henry, the vacuum.

He points his nozzle towards the floor. He clearly disapproves.

"Listen! It's obvious the pills aren't doing the trick. And I'm already on the maximum dosage. I needed to take situations into my own hands."

"But there are programs for this sort of thing," says the carpet sucker.

"Yeah, but not in this state. And fuck the man! I'm not paying taxes on this shit."

"We are aware of the fact that we're talking to a household appliance," says my brain, audibly.

"Yes, brain. We are aware of this."

I look down at the little bag containing my new "prescription."

"Hmm...," I say.

"A problem?" asks Henry.

"I think this batch is laced with something."

"How can you tell?" asks the inanimate object.

"You just answered your own question."

"How so?"

"You suck dirt! You shouldn't be able to talk. Let alone have a conversation with me."

"Na, see, I'm one of those new talking vacuums with a functioning brain and whatnot."

"Bull."

"No, totally. You just bought me the other day."

"Like fun I did. You're like six years old."

"And yesterday was my birthday!"

"You don't have one of those!"

"Are you saying I just magically appeared out of thin air? Do you know how re-goddamned-diculous that sounds?"

"As a matter of fact, I do. I'm talking to a FUCKING VACUUM!"

"Such childish behavior," says my brain, now floating around the room.

"Would you get back in my head!" I yell.

"Make me," it says.

"I'll show you who's a fucking vacuum," says Henry, raising his nozzle towards my mind.

"What are you doing?" I ask, knowing exactly what it is that bastard hoover is thinking.

"Hey, what are you doing?" asks my brain.

"Don't worry!" I shout over the loud sucking noise coming from Henry. My ass he's not a vacuum. I know a vacuum when I see one.

I run into the kitchen and swing open the refrigerator door. I don't know why I'm looking for a weapon in here, but I'm here now so I might as well look around.

I grab the whipped cream can and with what I could only assume is a mischievous glint in my eye I race back to the cleaning tool that's trying to devour my brain.

I pop the cap and bellow, "Take this, you... object!"

I press the button on the top of the canister and out shoots a cold stream of justice in the form of a whip. I snag Henry with my whipped cream whip and drag him closer to me. This is made exceedingly easy due the wheels Henry has screwed into his butt.

"If you haven't been sent here to clean up after me then why do you have this really long hose, wheels on your ass and are incredibly talented at sucking for hours on end."

Henry looks at me with his cold, lifeless attachments and says, "Because I'm a very generous and thoughtful lover."

I break the whip off the end of the canister, unclog my brain from the end of Henry's supposed mouth-tube or whatever and start spraying gallons of milky-white foam down his throat, I guess.

Henry collapses and spurts out some of the chilly dessert topping which magically floats away.

As my brain returns to my skull I look at the label of my trusty weapon.

"Huh. Didn't know that that's what they meant by 'Light.'"

WHIP

Do I go to the store?
  Do I stay in?
  Do I go to the store?
  Do I stay in?
  I technically have enough food to make it through the day. Of course some of that means eating expired milk in my cereal. I could skip the cereal and just have... Nothing as it would seem. Dry cereal works. And the marshmallow pieces are even better without milk. Especially rancid milk.
  But if I went to the store I could get other things as well. Some type of sleep-aid would be nice. Or a shit-ton of alcohol would probably do the trick right about now. Maybe something to induce a carbohydrate coma. Pasta might do it. Or cookies! No, wait. Bagels. Toast a couple of those tasty bastards up, slather them with butter and watch the sheep come bounding over my bed.
  That's it. I'm putting this to a vote. All those in favor of me going to the store and attempting to be a contributing

member of society, at least in an economic sense please say I.

"I," I say out-loud to reinforce the idea that this happened to be a good one.

All those opposed?

No.

That was odd.

"Is there someone else in here?"

I wait for the voice to come back, but there's just silence.

Fantastic. I thought this medication was supposed to stop me from being crazy. No, no. Get it out of your head. It was probably someone turning on their TV and not realizing that it was on super loud. That had to be it. Happy thoughts. I can do this.

I'm doing it. I'm walking to the store. Thankfully it's just a couple minutes down the road and not this epic quest. No thank you.

People pass by and I try to conceal my hands so my panic tremors don't show. It doesn't really work. I can tell that they see it. It's almost like I can hear their thoughts. They probably think I'm some raving drug addict coming off a bender. To be fair, I am on plenty of things that I probably could have a good time if things got desperate.

I reach the store and cautiously enter through the automatic doors. I really should have looked at the time before leaving because it seems like everyone is here getting their lunches. Plus there's a ton of teenagers. Is today a holiday or something? Fuck, I really didn't think this through all the way.

Nope.

Who the hell said that? I wasn't talking out-loud then was I? It's okay. Keep it together. Pick up a basket, get supplies and get the fuck out.

I start looking through the pre-made sandwiches, then the drinks, followed by the bakery.

Should probably pick up some fruit. Vitamins and stuff. I quickly turn back around to head towards the fresh fruit section when I accidentally bump into a very large man holding what I could only assume is the last bottle of olives. I assume this because of his reaction to me colliding into him, which is then immediately followed by him dropping the disgusting balls of ick and the glass bottle shattering as it hits the floor.

Plus the words he uses to describe my dumbassery really put the whole thing into perspective. But then, wouldn't you know it, that sets me off and I start shaking like a Torontonian prostitute in January. This leads me to knock into a couple other customers who also happen to be holding things that can break and they do.

Here I am, standing in the middle of the biggest clusterfuck since George W. Bush's brilliant idea to help the Iraqi citizens out by bombing the shit out of them, when the manager comes over. He sees me, spazing out like a meth addict watching Breaking Bad, and everyone else giving me nastier looks than the Smith family gave Miley.

And now I'm outside said store with more than just my ego bruised. Looks like it's dry cereal after all. Really rethinking taking this walk.

Told you.

ZEST

My doctor is going on about something. I should probably be paying attention to this. I'm sure it'll have something to do with my panic attacks. Damn things really toast my... buns? Eh, who knows.

"So you got all that?" he says.

"Yep."

He looks at me the way I look at peas. Or green beans. Or brussels sprouts. Or, well, pretty much any vegetable. He clearly knows I haven't been paying attention, but I just want to get out of here and back onto the couch with my good friends Bob, Sterling, Fry and Roger.

"And you'll let me know if you're hearing any more voices?" he says. "That's probably a sign that we need to adjust your medication."

"No problem," I say. And it wouldn't be, except for the fact that I kind of like them. They keep me company on those long winter nights in the fields. Hey, I'm just as confused as you are, but I feel good so fuck it. "Anything else I should know?"

"Just take it easy. Nothing too strenuous."

"I don't think that will be a problem. I just signed up to one of those streaming video services and I plan on getting my eight bucks worth and then some."

"Well you sound like you got things all figured out. I'd like to see you in a month to see how you're doing."

"And my friend wants to bang Kirsten Dunst, but I doubt Little Miss Chiclet-Teeth will be calling anytime soon."

"Pardon?"

"French?"

"You might want to get that prescription filled sooner rather than later. You're train-of-thought seems a bit..."

"Lemony?" I suggest.

"Sure, why not."

The pharmacy is packed. Just like my colon. I knew I should have stopped off at Burritos Burritos Burritos after coming here. But no! I had have six sopapillas.

I get on line and wait my turn. It's now a race between my ever-widening anus and the pharmacist. Just three people in front of me. I can do this. Wait! I forgot to factor in the time it'll take to talk to her. Plus the time to find a toilet afterwards. Shit. I think I may have to change my plans unless I want to change my pants. Not to mention the line forming behind me. Anxiety is like the worst thing for your bowels. Yeah. I'm going to have to make a break for it.

I dart from the line and make my way down a couple isles only knocking over three elderly women – A new record! – run out the exit and around to the back of the building. I drop my pants and proceed to fertilize the pavement.

"Nice butthole!" says a voice I hear coming from the wall behind me.

Marvelous! Either the store is talking to me or I'm hearing disembodied voices. I guess they both would be disembodied voices since stores don't have bodies. Well, they do in a ways. There's people in them and they have bodies. But what if they didn't? What if they just had heads with arms and legs flopping around? I have to remember to look that shit up on the internet when I get home.

"Hey!," says the strange voice.

"What?" I yell to no one in particular. Or the building itself. I don't know, I'm not well.

"Stop pooping on our wall!"

Holy crap on a biscotti, the store is sentient. I knew it!

"You have eyes?" I ask.

"There's a fucking camera looking right at you!" it says.

"Well aren't you saucy!"

"No, seriously! Stop taking a dump on the store!"

"Ugh! I hate it when stores refer to themselves in the third person."

"Listen, fucknuts! You're pooping on the store and we can see you thanks to the cameras we have set up in what we like to call the drive-thru prescription window."

Shit.

After a quick visit from the police, I'm on my way home with my medication. Thankfully I was just let off with a warning since this was my first offense and they took into account the massive amounts of Sertraline and Clonazepam I'm currently taking.

The good news is I'm fucking calm as shit now. You could smack me in the junk with a weed whacker a dozen or so times and I would not give a flying fuck. And speaking of weed, that helps too!

The bad news is I'm running out of food and in no way shape or form fit enough to leave... well this couch actually. I have the strangest feeling my motor skills might be

slightly impaired. But of all the bad news in the world, I'd say this is pretty low on the list.

FRAY

Gotta get up for work. Gotta get up for work. Gotta get up for work. Gotta get up for work. Gotta get up for work. Gotta get up for work. Gotta get up for work. Gotta get up for work.

Really need to get up for work. Really need to get up for work. Really need to get up for work. Really need to get up for work. Really need to get up for work. Really need to get up for work. Really need to get up for work. Really need to get up for work. Really need to get up for work.

Shower time. Shower time. I can do this. Shower time. Shower time. I can totally do this. Shower time. A little shaky. Shower time.

"Hi penis!"

Brush the teeth. Brush the teeth. Easy. No problem. Shaking actually helps with this one. Don't throw up.

Put on work clothes. Put on work clothes. Put on work clothes. Too much. How about boxers? Put on boxers. Put on boxers. Put on boxers. Okay. Boxers are on. Socks. Putting on the socks. Socks go on feet. Feet meet socks.

Nervous tick. Right on schedule! Still making good time. Alright pants. I hate you. Pants on the legs. Putting on pants. Putting on pants. Not putting on pants. Sitting down. Going too fast. Ease into this.

Take two. Trying pants yet again. Legs go in the pants. One at a time. Pants go on legs. Friends. Pants. Pants. Pants are on. Belt! Where's that belt? Belt? The fuck, belt?

"Where's my goddamned fucking belt," I scream as I slam my fist into the wardrobe door. Clothing flies everywhere. My rage builds to a violent peak. I remember to breathe.

Late. Panic. Frantic text to manager. Feel the judgment through the phone. Find belt.

Buttoning up shirt. Buttoning up shirt. Buttoning up shirt. Cat hair everywhere. Lint roller under bed. Hand spazing out in an attempt to peel off dirty sheet. Roll myself up and down.

Walk into the kitchen. Grab a water. Take some pills. Walk out door. Walk out door. Walk out door. Walk out door. Walk out door. Punch door. Walk out door. Out of door. Lock apartment. Apartment locked.

Walking to work. Walking to work. Walking to work. People everywhere. They're all looking at me. Walking to work. No matter what street I take there's always someone there. Friends at work. Walk to friends. Walk to friends. Too crowded. Need to hide. Need to hide. Hiding. Hiding. People still walking passed. I can feel them spying on me.

"F-f-f-fuck. L-l-l-leave me a-a-a-lone!"

More people stare. Get to work. Safe at work. Get to work. Safe at work. Keep head down. Keep head down. Get to work. Safe.

Calming down. Friends are here. Taking another pill. Relax. Everything's okay. Just like every other day.

Shop's incredibly busy. There are customer's everywhere. One leaves two more come in. Absolute Hell. I'm here at the till just waiting for the next problem.

A gentleman approaches. The transaction is taking place. He's attempting to make small talk with me. I mess something up on the computer. I need to see his bank card again. He's not too happy.

"Why?" he asks.

"I did something out of order so I need to swipe it again." I respond truthfully.

"What did you fuck up?"

I love it when they curse at us.

"Uh," I start.

"You're not going to charge me twice, are you?"

"Of course not."

"If there's a second charge I'm going to come back in here and knock you the fuck out."

Jesus! I'm in my thirties and I still get talked to like this. The panic starts to set in again. My hands start shaking erratically. Co-workers come by to make sure I'm okay. I leave and head into the back office. Embarrassed beyond belief. Everyone saw that. Everyone thinks I'm a joke.

I'm told to go home. It's obvious that I'll be no help here. I begin my walk of shame back to my apartment. Everyone has to work harder now because of me. I fail them yet again.

BALANCE

There's a stillness in the air that whispers contentment. Every day should be like this day. My girlfriend and I are sitting on the couch reading a couple of books we picked up at the charity shop down the street. One of our cats in on my lap and the other is sitting between us. He's a fat little bastard so he likes his own cushion.

It's warm outside so our windows are open. It's surprisingly silent in the city. Everyone seems to be enjoying the rare blue sky and sun.

There's freshly-baked banana bread cooling on the counter. Dinner tonight is a margarita pizza from the Italian restaurant on the ground floor of our building. And for dessert? Stracciatella gelato.

I'm sufficiently medicated for all of today's activities. Which will essentially be books, food and television. I don't have to leave the house for anything until three days from now. And I most likely won't.

It already haunts me though. Every night, I lay awake dreading the impending doom up ahead. It rarely happens

right away. I'll usually just be there, trying to fall asleep and a random thought will slither into my head. It's most likely something about the future that could potentially happen. Or something in the distance that I know is there, but there are many ways for said situation to play out.

I'll try putting on my headphones and listening to some music. That's a tricky one too. Do I listen to something I know really well and risk my mind drifting and all of a sudden I'm in the midst of a full-blown panic attack without even realizing it? Or do I play something new that I don't know? If I do the latter I'll most likely be awake through the entire album because of how much attention I was giving each song; all the while not any closer to dreamland. Repeat ad infinitum.

Perhaps I'll get up and watch television, but again. The same concerns apply while adding to my sleep deprivation. Not to mention the crippling depression. Or the delusional behavior. Then the inevitable mood swing to hating just about everything and getting irritated by the most infinitesimal annoyance and not being able to do a single thing about anything. Then finally winding up in a fetal position on the floor as my limbs spasm out of control. I try to regain composure, but the only action I manage to muster is hitting myself or my surroundings as some form of distraction.

Eventually it subsides and I'm exhausted. Sleep comes almost immediately after laying back down in bed. It's reached the point where I almost expect this type of thing to happen every night. I'm so drained that I sleep most of the morning away, don't leave the house during the day and then have too much energy built up in me to sleep the next night. Everyone says to meditate or exercise, but those things just let the mind wander causing more trouble.

That is, unless I catch it in time and pop a pill to numb everything.

As far as I can tell there's no escape from the fear of the unknown. Except..., but even that has its own horror attached. The only way forward is to fight and hope that someday these feelings won't be a part of me anymore. Until then?

I hope.

Acknowledgements

I'd just like to thank my family and friends for being so understanding during this time and in the future as I try to get better.

About the Author

Stephen Schwegler thinks there's enough about him already in this book and doesn't feel like adding anything else. If you want to know more, and who could blame you, please visit www.stephenschwegler.com. He's also on social media, but doesn't post much. He's sorry about that, but doesn't intend on doing a damn thing about it.

Thanks.